BLACK SQUADRON: VOLUME 2

It has been thirty years since the defeat of the Empire, but a new threat has arrived. General Leia Organa is leading the Resistance to keep the First Order at bay.

Leia has tasked star pilot Poe Dameron with finding Lor San Tekka – an explorer who may know the location of Luke Skywalker. Poe has assembled a team of pilots – Black Squadron – and together they have set off to the explorer's last known whereabouts: a planet whose residents worship and care for a massive egg.

Meanwhile, Poe's droid, BB-8, has discovered a tracker on Poe's X-wing, a tracker Poe believes was placed there by the First Order. Poe's suspicions are proven correct when he discovers the enemy is closer than anticipated....

CHARLES SOULE
Writer

PHIL NOTO
Artist

VC's JOE CARAMAGNA
Letterer

PHIL NOTO
Cover Artist

HEATHER ANTOS
Assistant Editor

JORDAN D. WHITE
Editor

C.B. CEBULSKI
Executive Editor

AXEL ALONSO
Editor In Chief

JOE QUESADA
Chief Creative Officer

DAN BUCKLEY
Publisher

For Lucasfilm:
Senior Editor FRANK PARISI
Creative Director MICHAEL SIGLAIN
Lucasfilm Story Group RAYNE ROBERTS, PABLO HIDALGO, LELAND CHEE, MATT MARTIN

ABDO
Spotlight

ABDOPUBLISHING.COM

Reinforced library bound edition published in 2018 by Spotlight,
a division of ABDO, PO Box 398166, Minneapolis, Minnesota 55439.
Spotlight produces high-quality reinforced library bound editions for
schools and libraries. Published by agreement with Marvel Characters, Inc.

Printed in the United States of America, North Mankato, Minnesota.
092017
012018

 THIS BOOK CONTAINS
RECYCLED MATERIALS

STAR WARS © & TM 2018 LUCASFILM LTD.

PUBLISHER'S CATALOGING-IN-PUBLICATION DATA

Names: Soule, Charles, author. | Noto, Phil, illustrator.
Title: Black Squadron / writer: Charles Soule ; art: Phil Noto.
Description: Minneapolis, MN : Spotlight, 2018 | Series: Star Wars: Poe Dameron
Summary: While exploring the last known location of an explorer for General Leia
    Organa, ace pilot Poe Dameron finds a tracking device on his ship and is
    trapped in a cavern by First Order intelligence officer Agent Terex, while a fleet
    of TIEs engage the rest of the Black Squadron in a deadly aerial battle.
Identifiers: LCCN 2017941920 | ISBN 9781532141348 (v.1 ; lib. bdg.) | ISBN
    9781532141355 (v.2 ; lib. bdg.) | ISBN 9781532141362 (v.3 ; lib. bdg.)
Subjects: LCSH: Star Wars (film)--Juvenile fiction. | Adventure and Adventurers--
    Juvenile fiction. | Graphic Novels--Juvenile fiction.
Classification: DDC 741.5--dc23
LC record available at http://lccn.loc.gov/2017941920

ABDO
Spotlight

A Division of ABDO
abdopublishing.com

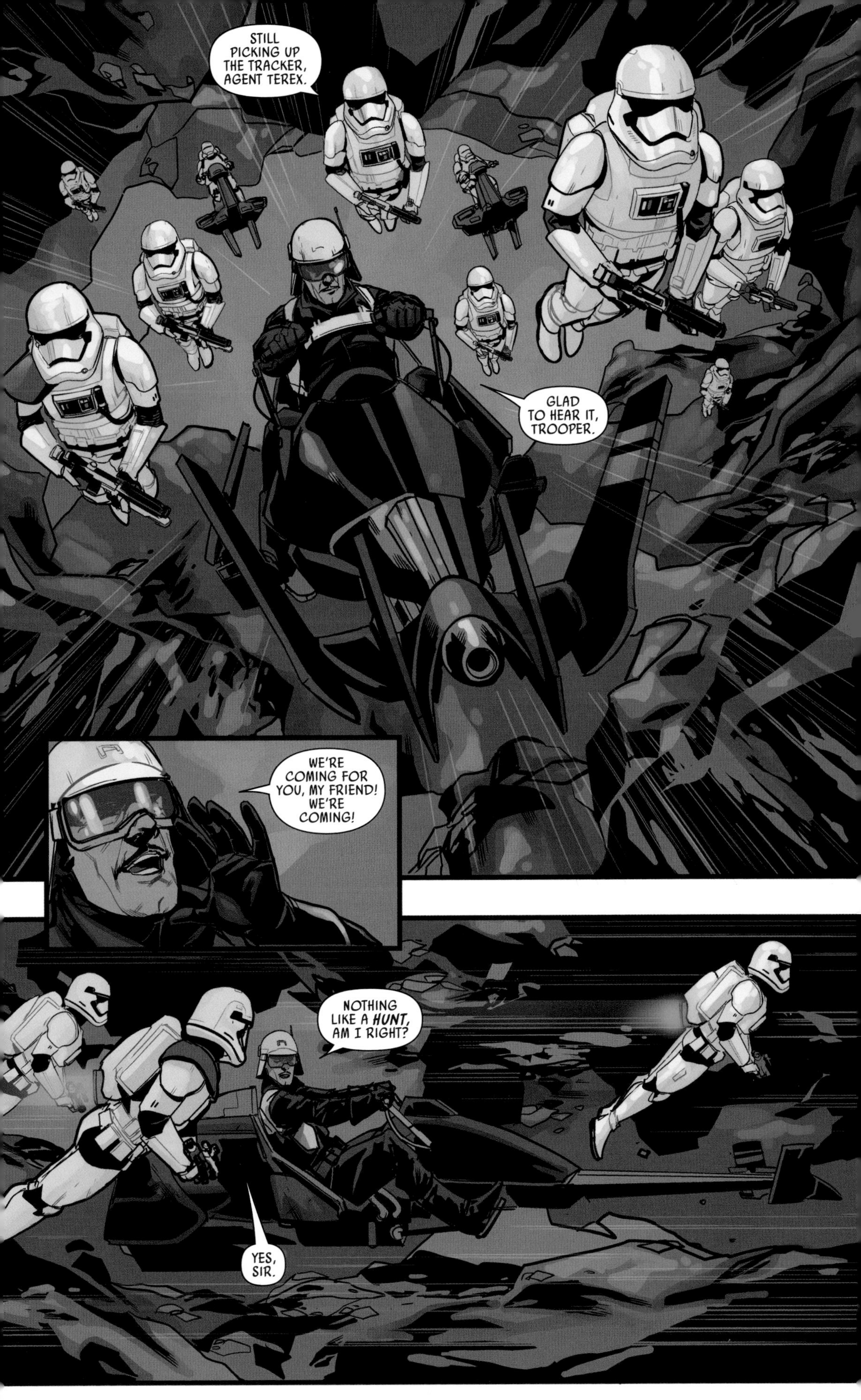
STILL PICKING UP THE TRACKER, AGENT TEREX.
GLAD TO HEAR IT, TROOPER.
WE'RE COMING FOR YOU, MY FRIEND! WE'RE COMING!
NOTHING LIKE A *HUNT*, AM I RIGHT?
YES, SIR.

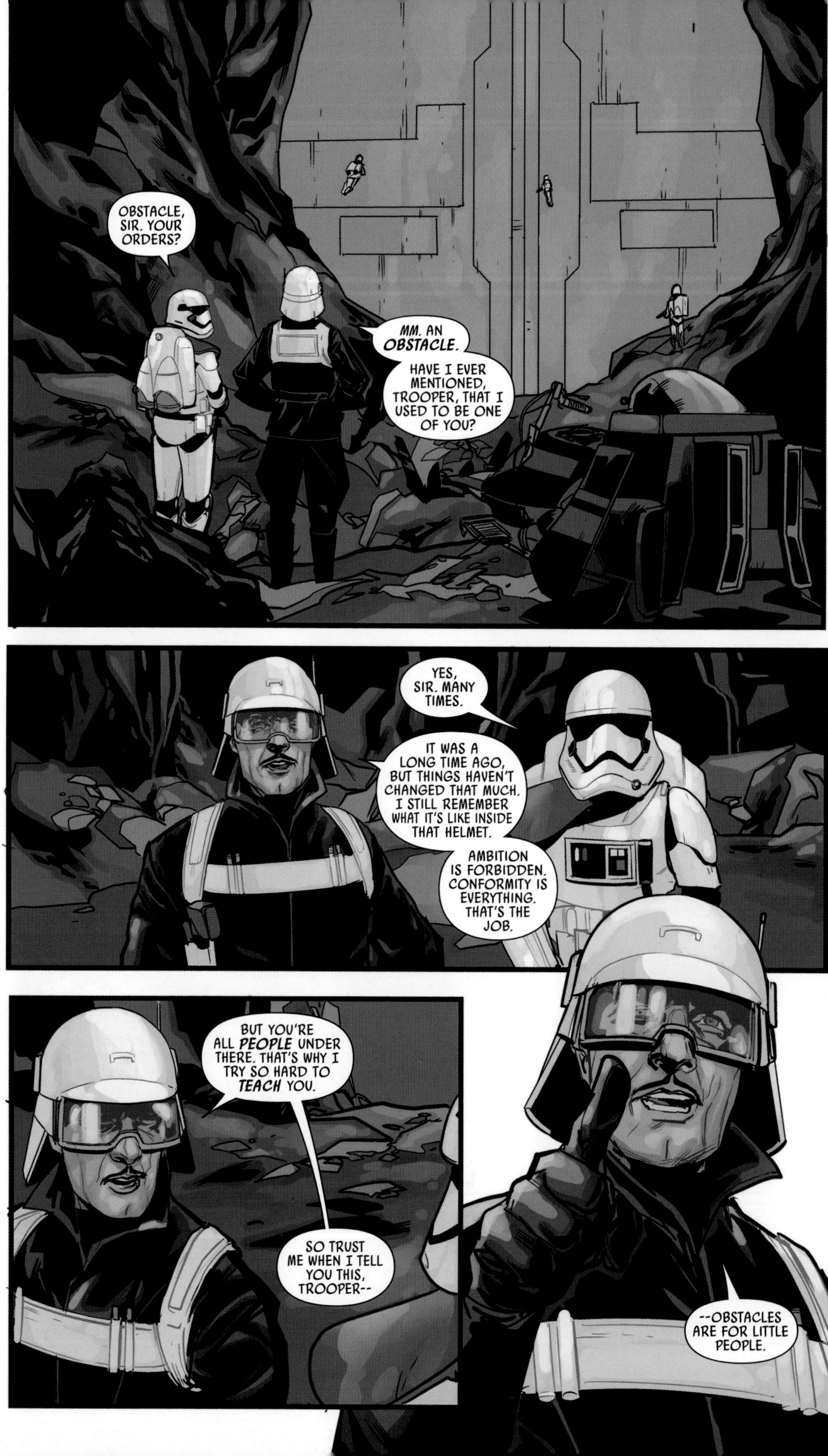
OBSTACLE, SIR. YOUR ORDERS?
MM. AN OBSTACLE.
HAVE I EVER MENTIONED, TROOPER, THAT I USED TO BE ONE OF YOU?
YES, SIR. MANY TIMES.
IT WAS A LONG TIME AGO, BUT THINGS HAVEN'T CHANGED THAT MUCH. I STILL REMEMBER WHAT IT'S LIKE INSIDE THAT HELMET.
AMBITION IS FORBIDDEN. CONFORMITY IS EVERYTHING. THAT'S THE JOB.
BUT YOU'RE ALL PEOPLE UNDER THERE. THAT'S WHY I TRY SO HARD TO TEACH YOU.
SO TRUST ME WHEN I TELL YOU THIS, TROOPER--
--OBSTACLES ARE FOR LITTLE PEOPLE.

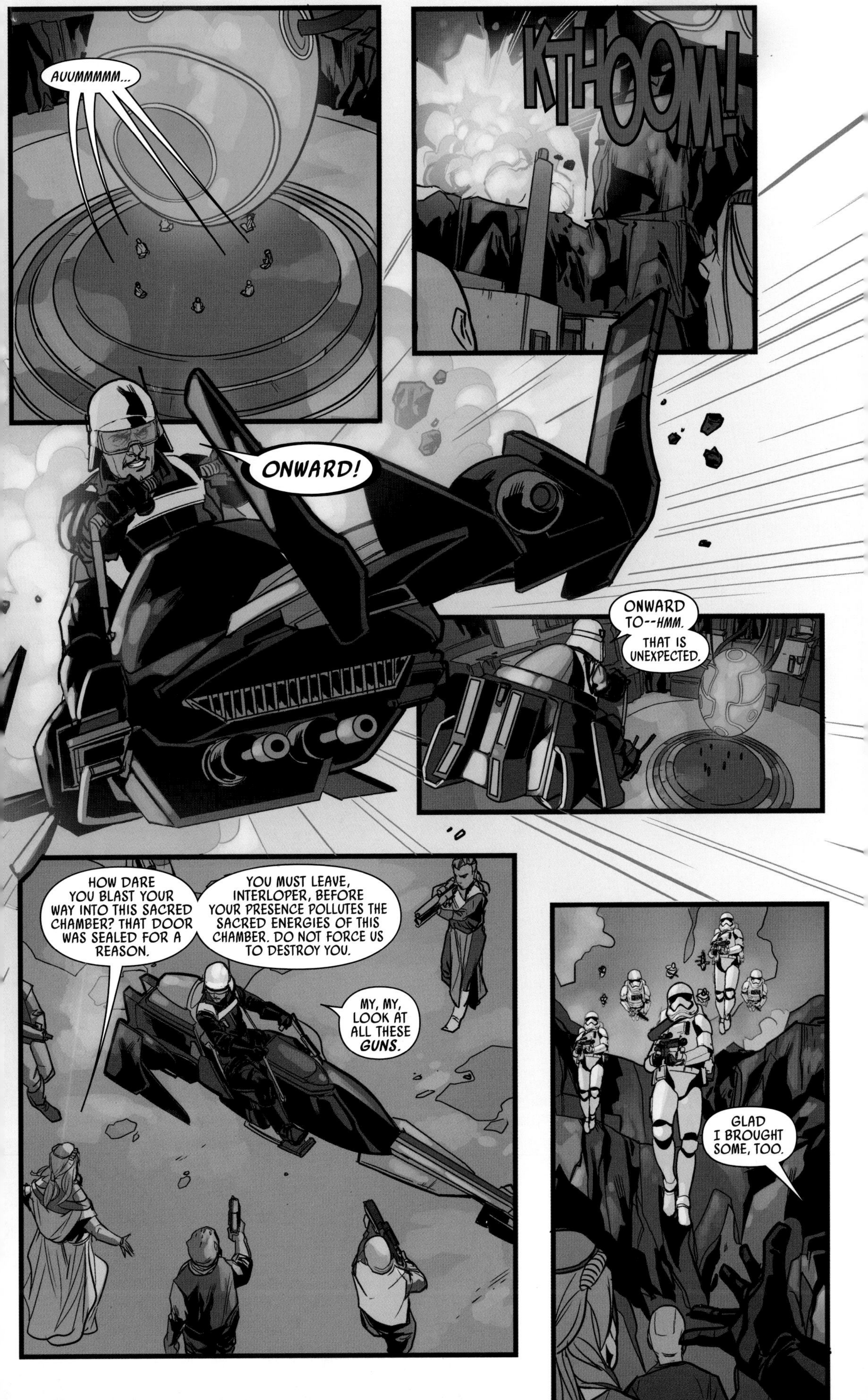
AUUMMMMM...
KTHOOM!
ONWARD!
ONWARD TO--HMM.
THAT IS UNEXPECTED.
HOW DARE YOU BLAST YOUR WAY INTO THIS SACRED CHAMBER? THAT DOOR WAS SEALED FOR A REASON.
YOU MUST LEAVE, INTERLOPER, BEFORE YOUR PRESENCE POLLUTES THE SACRED ENERGIES OF THIS CHAMBER. DO NOT FORCE US TO DESTROY YOU.
MY, MY, LOOK AT ALL THESE GUNS.
GLAD I BROUGHT SOME, TOO.

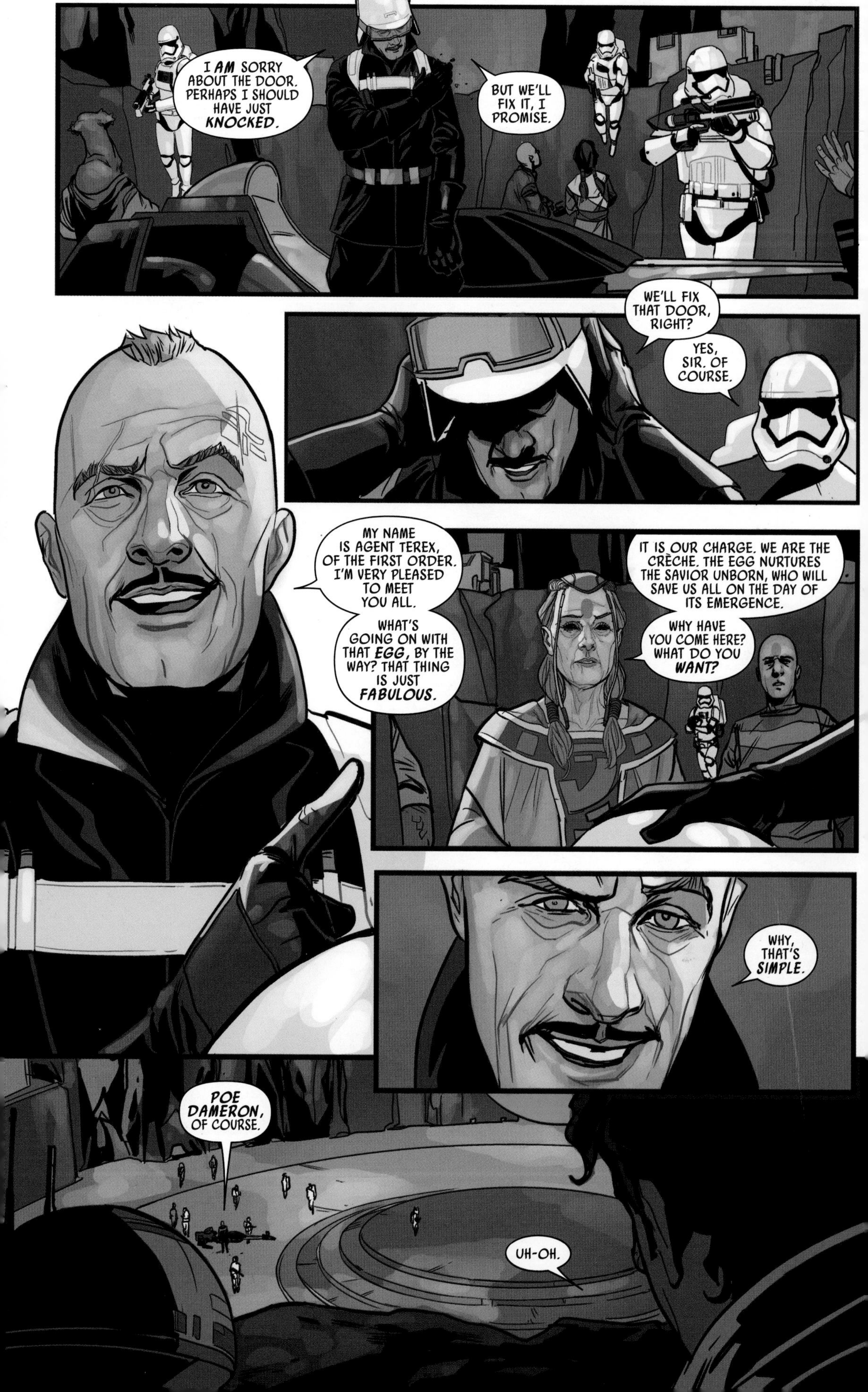
I AM SORRY ABOUT THE DOOR. PERHAPS I SHOULD HAVE JUST KNOCKED.
BUT WE'LL FIX IT, I PROMISE.
WE'LL FIX THAT DOOR, RIGHT?
YES, SIR. OF COURSE.
MY NAME IS AGENT TEREX, OF THE FIRST ORDER. I'M VERY PLEASED TO MEET YOU ALL.
WHAT'S GOING ON WITH THAT EGG, BY THE WAY? THAT THING IS JUST FABULOUS.
IT IS OUR CHARGE. WE ARE THE CRÈCHE. THE EGG NURTURES THE SAVIOR UNBORN, WHO WILL SAVE US ALL ON THE DAY OF ITS EMERGENCE.
WHY HAVE YOU COME HERE? WHAT DO YOU WANT?
WHY, THAT'S SIMPLE.
POE DAMERON, OF COURSE.
UH-OH.

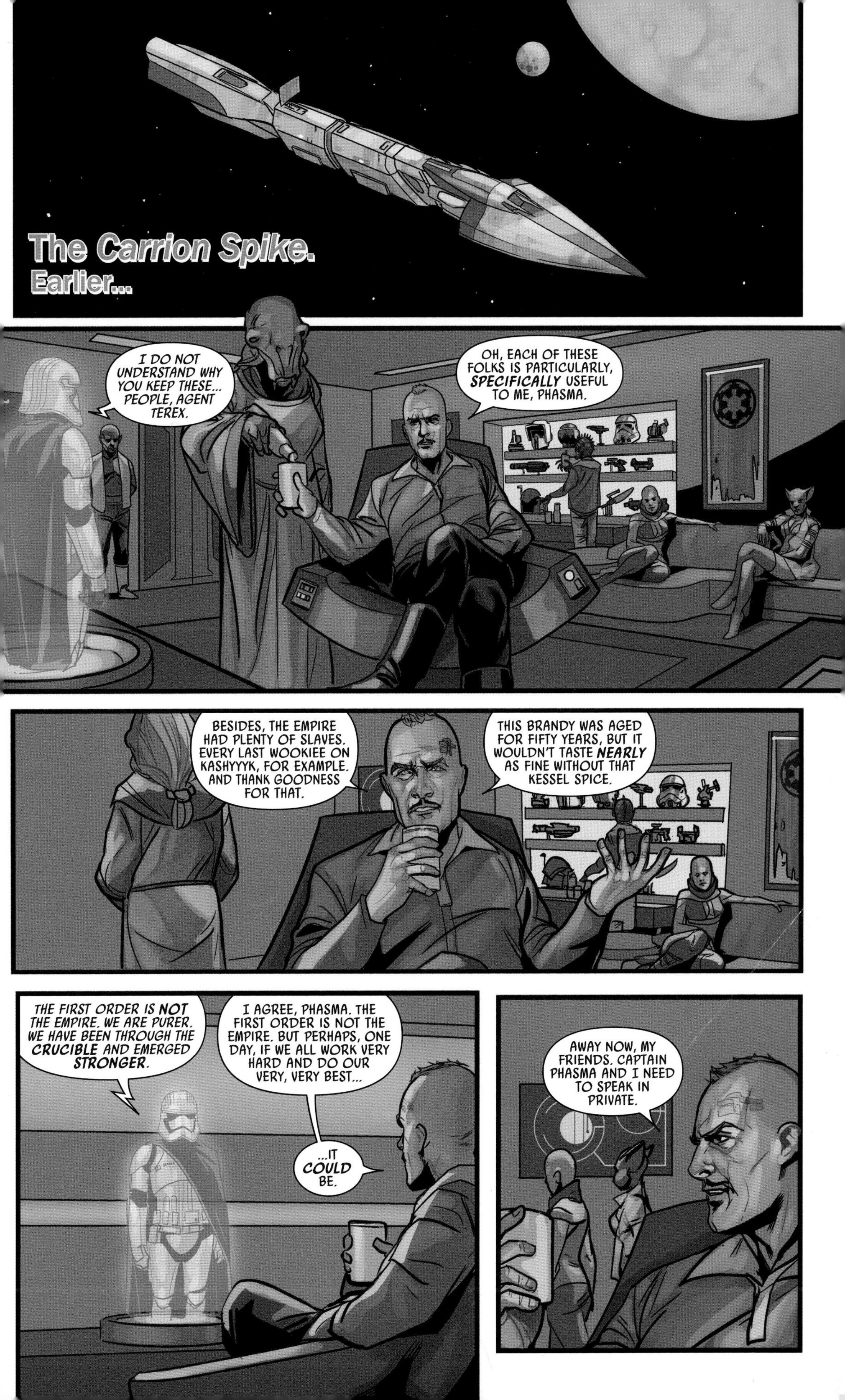
The Carrion Spike.
Earlier...
I DO NOT UNDERSTAND WHY YOU KEEP THESE... PEOPLE, AGENT TEREX.
OH, EACH OF THESE FOLKS IS PARTICULARLY, SPECIFICALLY USEFUL TO ME, PHASMA.
BESIDES, THE EMPIRE HAD PLENTY OF SLAVES. EVERY LAST WOOKIEE ON KASHYYYK, FOR EXAMPLE. AND THANK GOODNESS FOR THAT.
THIS BRANDY WAS AGED FOR FIFTY YEARS, BUT IT WOULDN'T TASTE NEARLY AS FINE WITHOUT THAT KESSEL SPICE.
THE FIRST ORDER IS NOT THE EMPIRE. WE ARE PURER. WE HAVE BEEN THROUGH THE CRUCIBLE AND EMERGED STRONGER.
I AGREE, PHASMA. THE FIRST ORDER IS NOT THE EMPIRE. BUT PERHAPS, ONE DAY, IF WE ALL WORK VERY HARD AND DO OUR VERY, VERY BEST...
...IT COULD BE.
AWAY NOW, MY FRIENDS. CAPTAIN PHASMA AND I NEED TO SPEAK IN PRIVATE.

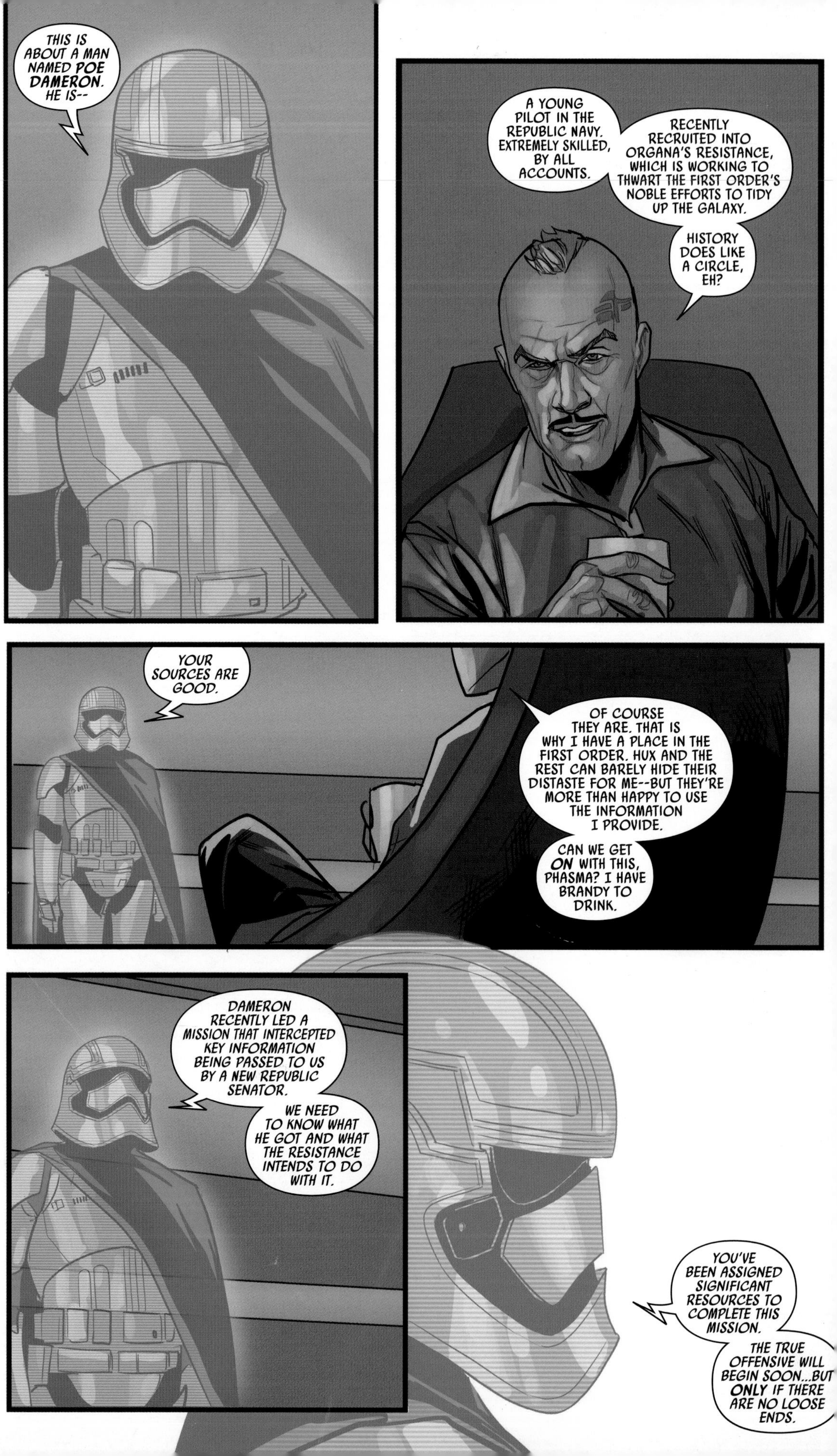
THIS IS ABOUT A MAN NAMED POE DAMERON. HE IS--
A YOUNG PILOT IN THE REPUBLIC NAVY. EXTREMELY SKILLED, BY ALL ACCOUNTS.
RECENTLY RECRUITED INTO ORGANA'S RESISTANCE, WHICH IS WORKING TO THWART THE FIRST ORDER'S NOBLE EFFORTS TO TIDY UP THE GALAXY.
HISTORY DOES LIKE A CIRCLE, EH?
YOUR SOURCES ARE GOOD.
OF COURSE THEY ARE. THAT IS WHY I HAVE A PLACE IN THE FIRST ORDER. HUX AND THE REST CAN BARELY HIDE THEIR DISTASTE FOR ME--BUT THEY'RE MORE THAN HAPPY TO USE THE INFORMATION I PROVIDE.
CAN WE GET ON WITH THIS, PHASMA? I HAVE BRANDY TO DRINK.
DAMERON RECENTLY LED A MISSION THAT INTERCEPTED KEY INFORMATION BEING PASSED TO US BY A NEW REPUBLIC SENATOR.
WE NEED TO KNOW WHAT HE GOT AND WHAT THE RESISTANCE INTENDS TO DO WITH IT.
YOU'VE BEEN ASSIGNED SIGNIFICANT RESOURCES TO COMPLETE THIS MISSION.
THE TRUE OFFENSIVE WILL BEGIN SOON...BUT ONLY IF THERE ARE NO LOOSE ENDS.

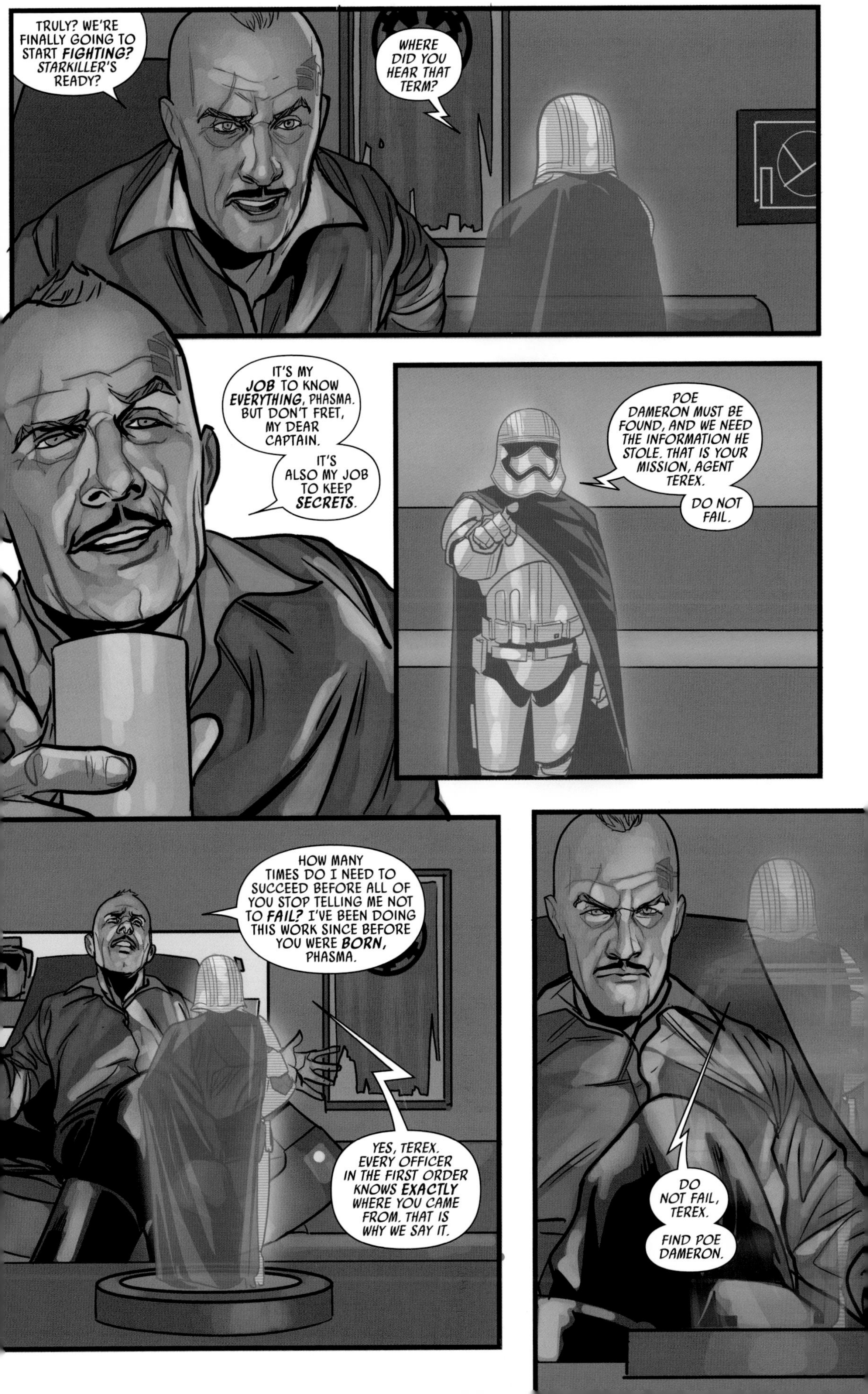
TRULY? WE'RE FINALLY GOING TO START FIGHTING? STARKILLER'S READY?
WHERE DID YOU HEAR THAT TERM?
IT'S MY JOB TO KNOW EVERYTHING, PHASMA. BUT DON'T FRET, MY DEAR CAPTAIN.
IT'S ALSO MY JOB TO KEEP SECRETS.
POE DAMERON MUST BE FOUND, AND WE NEED THE INFORMATION HE STOLE. THAT IS YOUR MISSION, AGENT TEREX.
DO NOT FAIL.
HOW MANY TIMES DO I NEED TO SUCCEED BEFORE ALL OF YOU STOP TELLING ME NOT TO FAIL? I'VE BEEN DOING THIS WORK SINCE BEFORE YOU WERE BORN, PHASMA.
YES, TEREX. EVERY OFFICER IN THE FIRST ORDER KNOWS EXACTLY WHERE YOU CAME FROM. THAT IS WHY WE SAY IT.
DO NOT FAIL, TEREX.
FIND POE DAMERON.

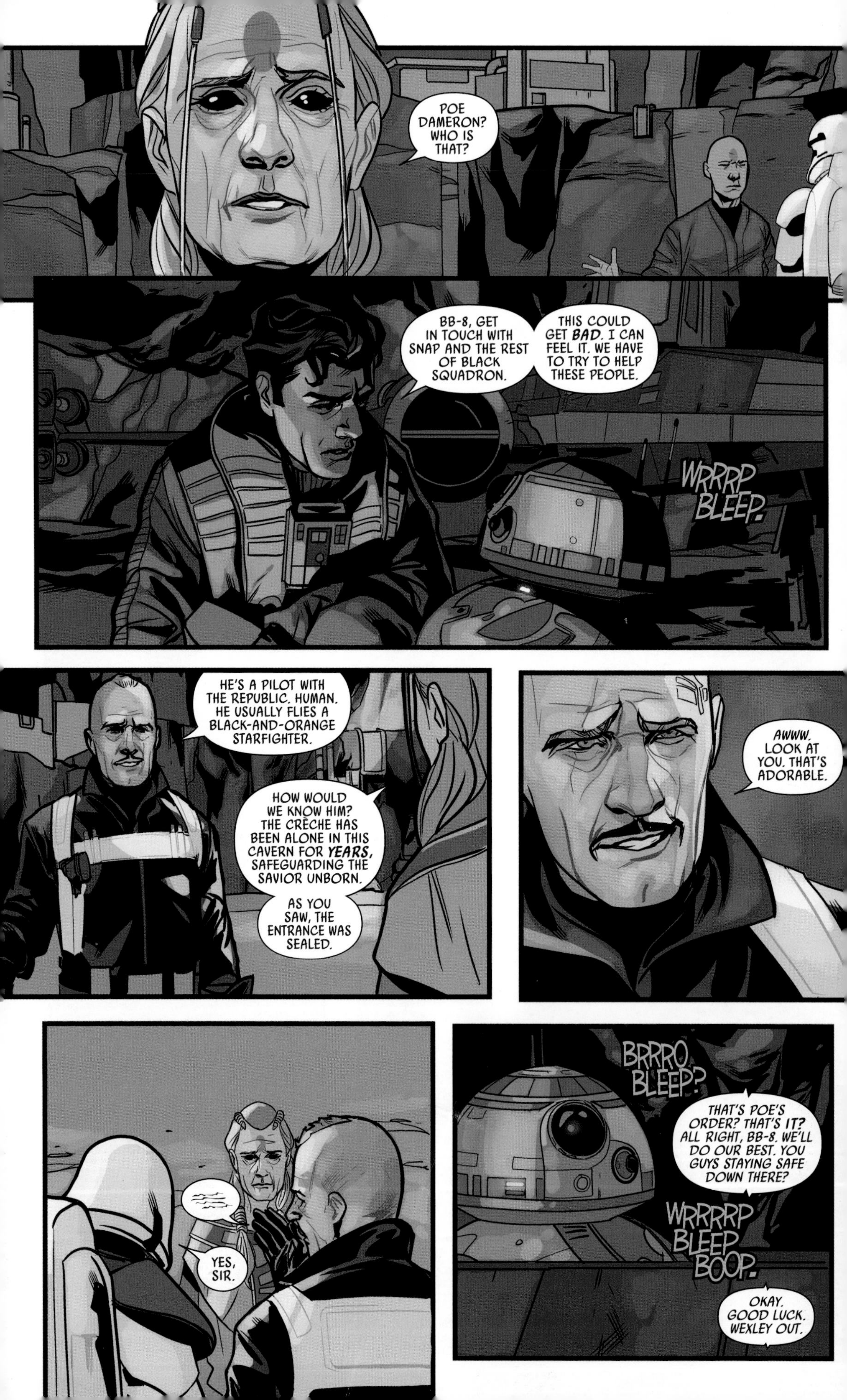
POE DAMERON? WHO IS THAT?
BB-8, GET IN TOUCH WITH SNAP AND THE REST OF BLACK SQUADRON.
THIS COULD GET BAD. I CAN FEEL IT. WE HAVE TO TRY TO HELP THESE PEOPLE.
WRRRP BLEEP.
HE'S A PILOT WITH THE REPUBLIC. HUMAN. HE USUALLY FLIES A BLACK-AND-ORANGE STARFIGHTER.
HOW WOULD WE KNOW HIM? THE CRÈCHE HAS BEEN ALONE IN THIS CAVERN FOR YEARS, SAFEGUARDING THE SAVIOR UNBORN.
AS YOU SAW, THE ENTRANCE WAS SEALED.
AWWW. LOOK AT YOU. THAT'S ADORABLE.
YES, SIR.
BRRRO BLEEP?
THAT'S POE'S ORDER? THAT'S IT? ALL RIGHT, BB-8. WE'LL DO OUR BEST. YOU GUYS STAYING SAFE DOWN THERE?
WRRRRP BLEEP BOOP.
OKAY. GOOD LUCK. WEXLEY OUT.

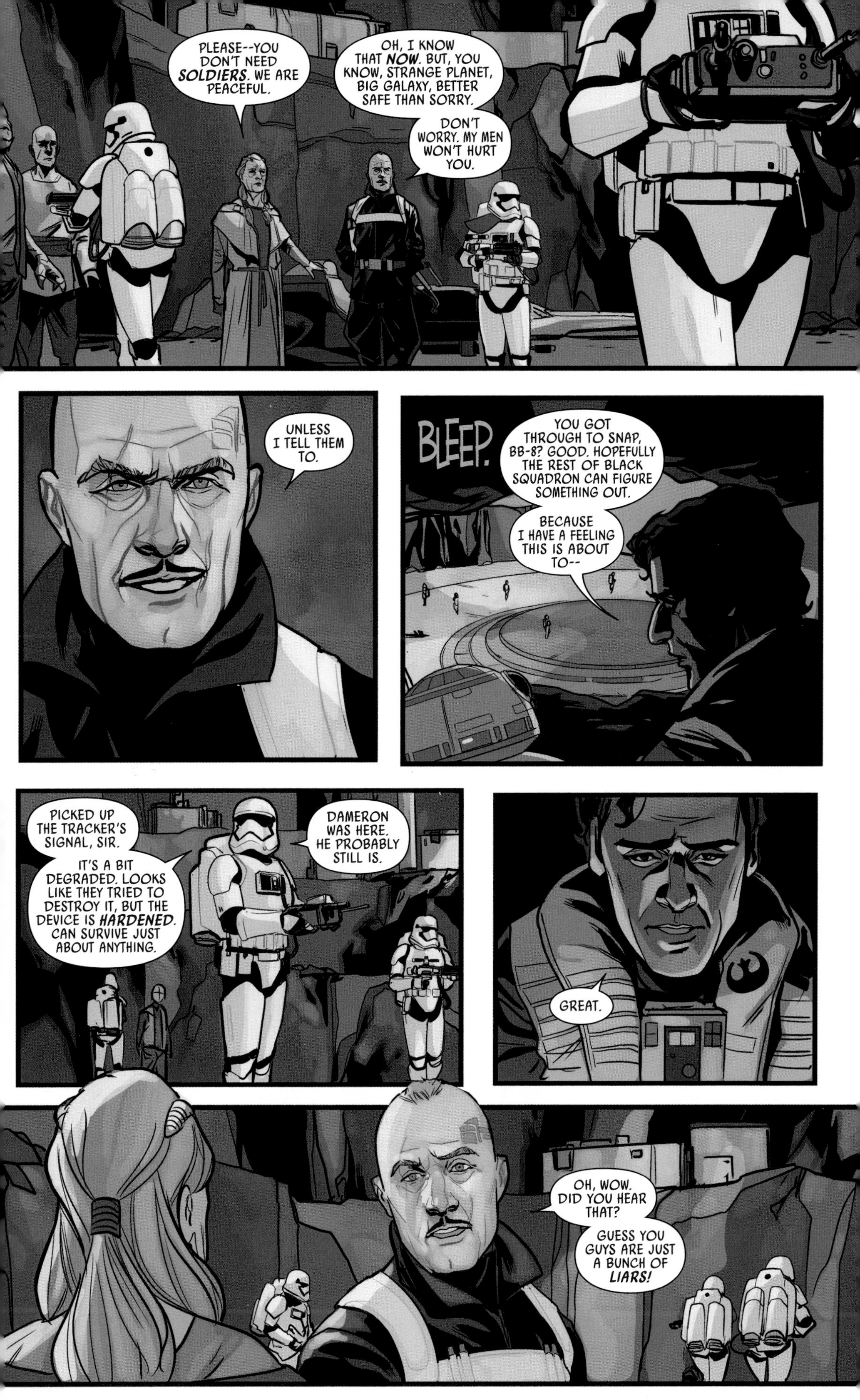

PLEASE--YOU DON'T NEED SOLDIERS. WE ARE PEACEFUL.
OH, I KNOW THAT NOW. BUT, YOU KNOW, STRANGE PLANET, BIG GALAXY, BETTER SAFE THAN SORRY.
DON'T WORRY. MY MEN WON'T HURT YOU.
UNLESS I TELL THEM TO.
BLEEP.
YOU GOT THROUGH TO SNAP, BB-8? GOOD. HOPEFULLY THE REST OF BLACK SQUADRON CAN FIGURE SOMETHING OUT.
BECAUSE I HAVE A FEELING THIS IS ABOUT TO--
PICKED UP THE TRACKER'S SIGNAL, SIR.
IT'S A BIT DEGRADED. LOOKS LIKE THEY TRIED TO DESTROY IT, BUT THE DEVICE IS HARDENED. CAN SURVIVE JUST ABOUT ANYTHING.
DAMERON WAS HERE. HE PROBABLY STILL IS.
GREAT.
OH, WOW. DID YOU HEAR THAT?
GUESS YOU GUYS ARE JUST A BUNCH OF LIARS!

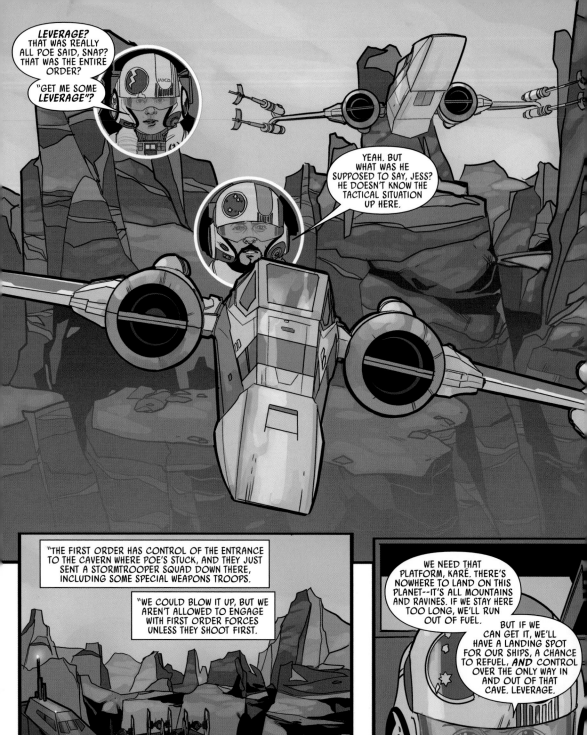

LEVERAGE? THAT WAS REALLY ALL POE SAID, SNAP? THAT WAS THE ENTIRE ORDER?

"GET ME SOME LEVERAGE"?

YEAH. BUT WHAT WAS HE SUPPOSED TO SAY, JESS? HE DOESN'T KNOW THE TACTICAL SITUATION UP HERE.

"THE FIRST ORDER HAS CONTROL OF THE ENTRANCE TO THE CAVERN WHERE POE'S STUCK, AND THEY JUST SENT A STORMTROOPER SQUAD DOWN THERE, INCLUDING SOME SPECIAL WEAPONS TROOPS.

"WE COULD BLOW IT UP, BUT WE AREN'T ALLOWED TO ENGAGE WITH FIRST ORDER FORCES UNLESS THEY SHOOT FIRST.

WE NEED THAT PLATFORM, KARÉ. THERE'S NOWHERE TO LAND ON THIS PLANET--IT'S ALL MOUNTAINS AND RAVINES. IF WE STAY HERE TOO LONG, WE'LL RUN OUT OF FUEL.

BUT IF WE CAN GET IT, WE'LL HAVE A LANDING SPOT FOR OUR SHIPS, A CHANCE TO REFUEL, AND CONTROL OVER THE ONLY WAY IN AND OUT OF THAT CAVE. LEVERAGE.

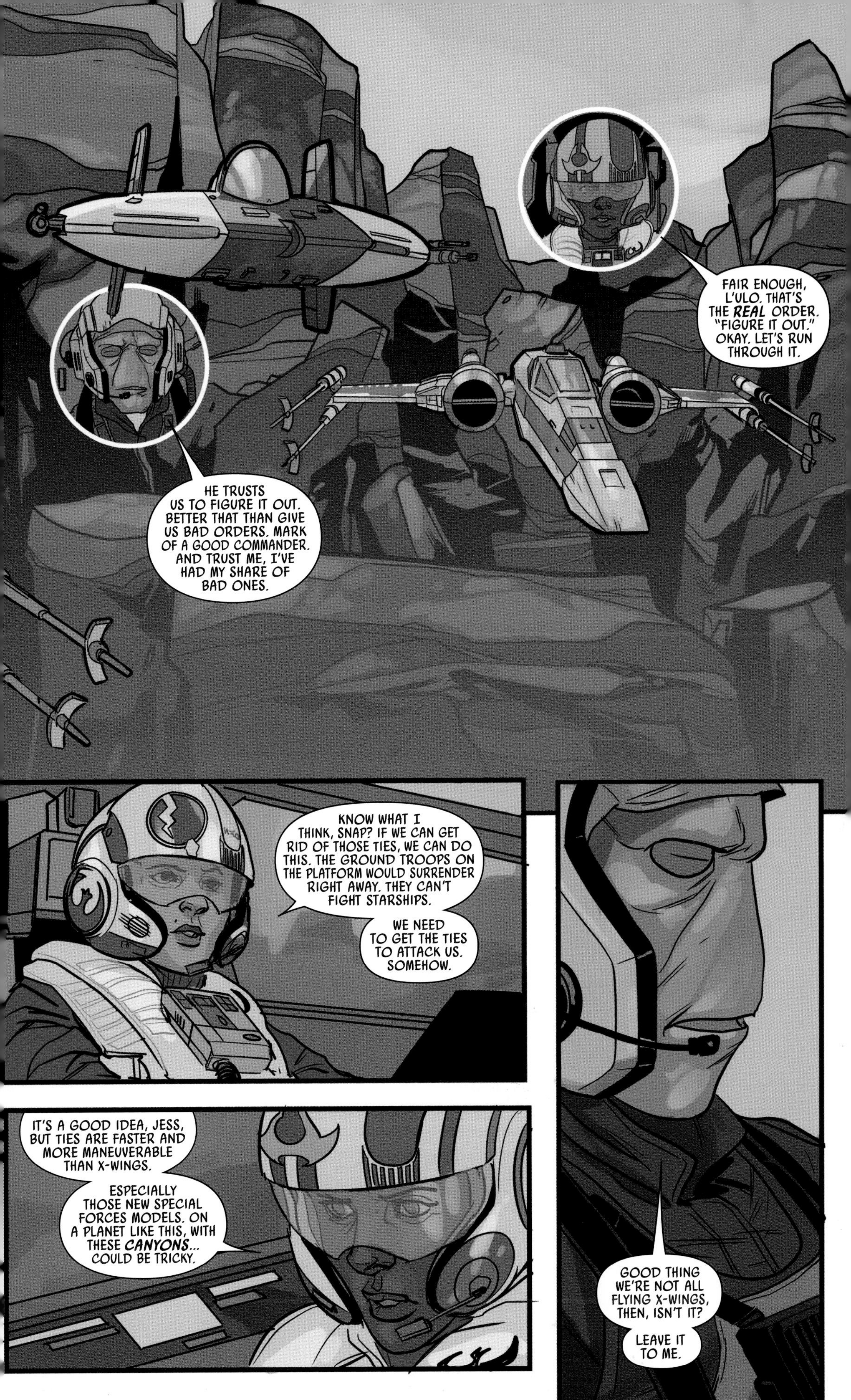
FAIR ENOUGH, L'ULO. THAT'S THE REAL ORDER. "FIGURE IT OUT." OKAY. LET'S RUN THROUGH IT.
HE TRUSTS US TO FIGURE IT OUT. BETTER THAT THAN GIVE US BAD ORDERS. MARK OF A GOOD COMMANDER. AND TRUST ME, I'VE HAD MY SHARE OF BAD ONES.
KNOW WHAT I THINK, SNAP? IF WE CAN GET RID OF THOSE TIES, WE CAN DO THIS. THE GROUND TROOPS ON THE PLATFORM WOULD SURRENDER RIGHT AWAY. THEY CAN'T FIGHT STARSHIPS.
WE NEED TO GET THE TIES TO ATTACK US. SOMEHOW.
IT'S A GOOD IDEA, JESS, BUT TIES ARE FASTER AND MORE MANEUVERABLE THAN X-WINGS.
ESPECIALLY THOSE NEW SPECIAL FORCES MODELS. ON A PLANET LIKE THIS, WITH THESE CANYONS... COULD BE TRICKY.
GOOD THING WE'RE NOT ALL FLYING X-WINGS, THEN, ISN'T IT?
LEAVE IT TO ME.

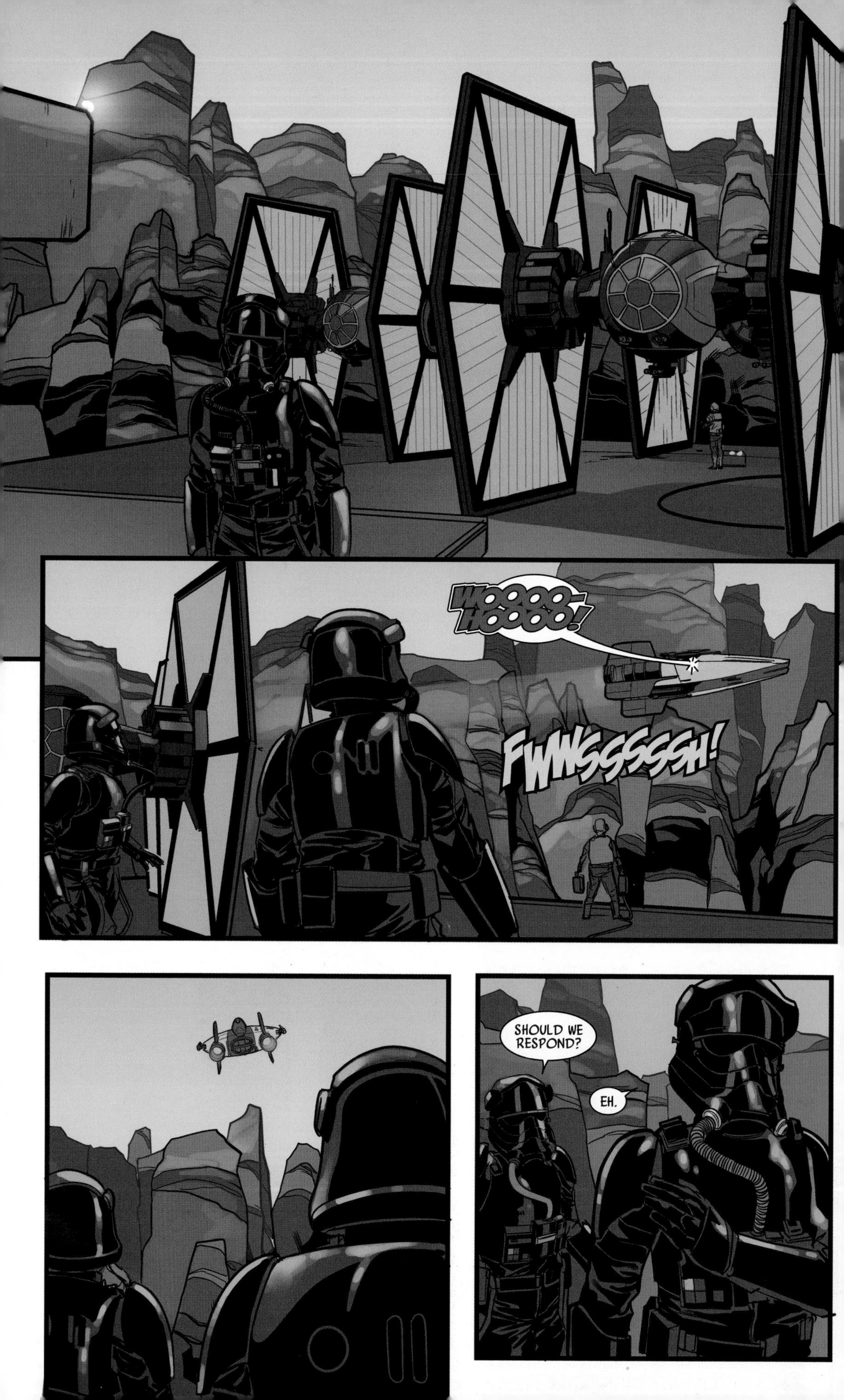
WOOOO-HOOOOO!
FWWSSSSSH!
SHOULD WE RESPOND?
EH.

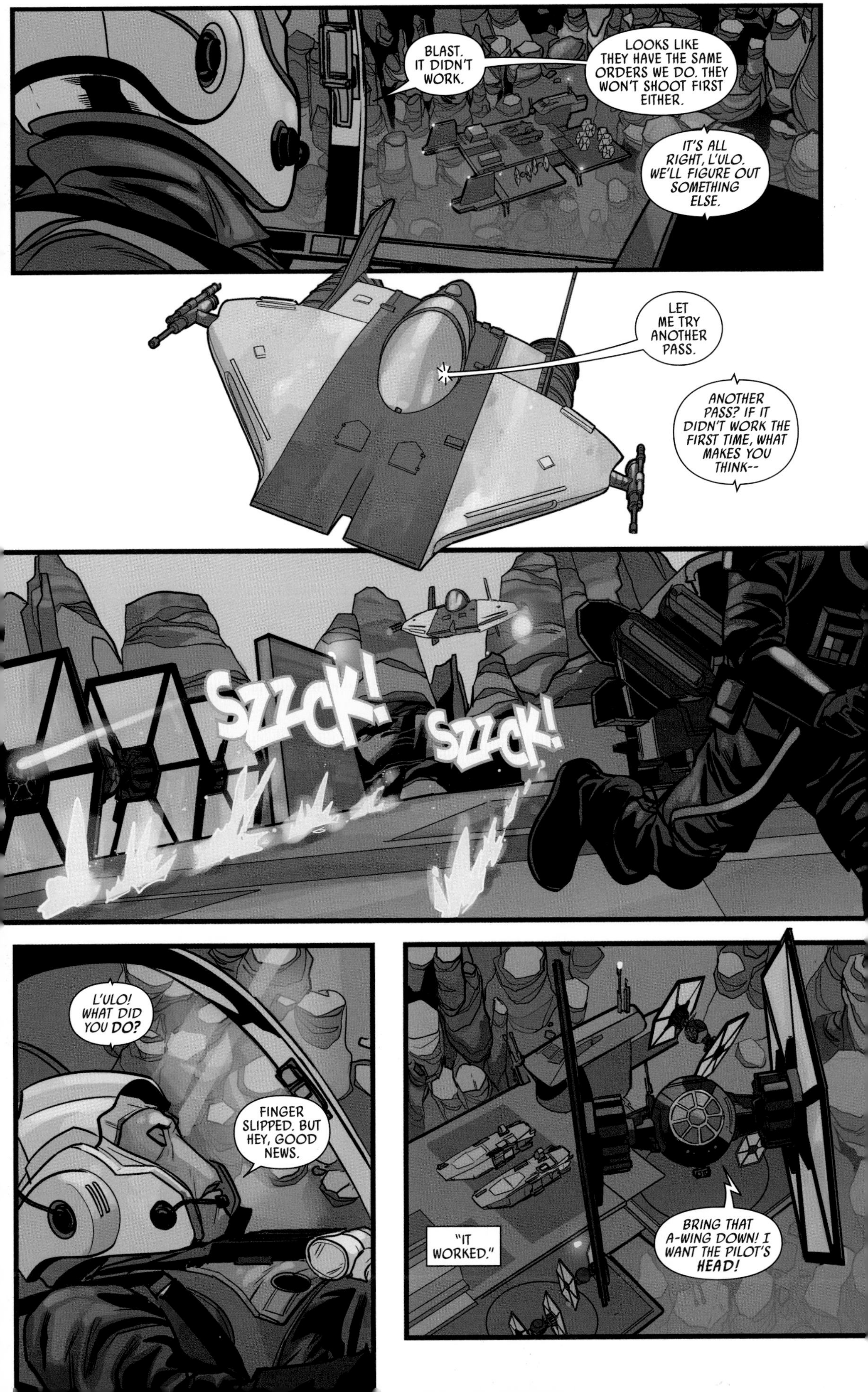
BLAST. IT DIDN'T WORK.
LOOKS LIKE THEY HAVE THE SAME ORDERS WE DO. THEY WON'T SHOOT FIRST EITHER.
IT'S ALL RIGHT, L'ULO. WE'LL FIGURE OUT SOMETHING ELSE.
LET ME TRY ANOTHER PASS.
ANOTHER PASS? IF IT DIDN'T WORK THE FIRST TIME, WHAT MAKES YOU THINK--
SZZCK!
SZZCK!
L'ULO! WHAT DID YOU DO?
FINGER SLIPPED. BUT HEY, GOOD NEWS.
"IT WORKED."
BRING THAT A-WING DOWN! I WANT THE PILOT'S HEAD!

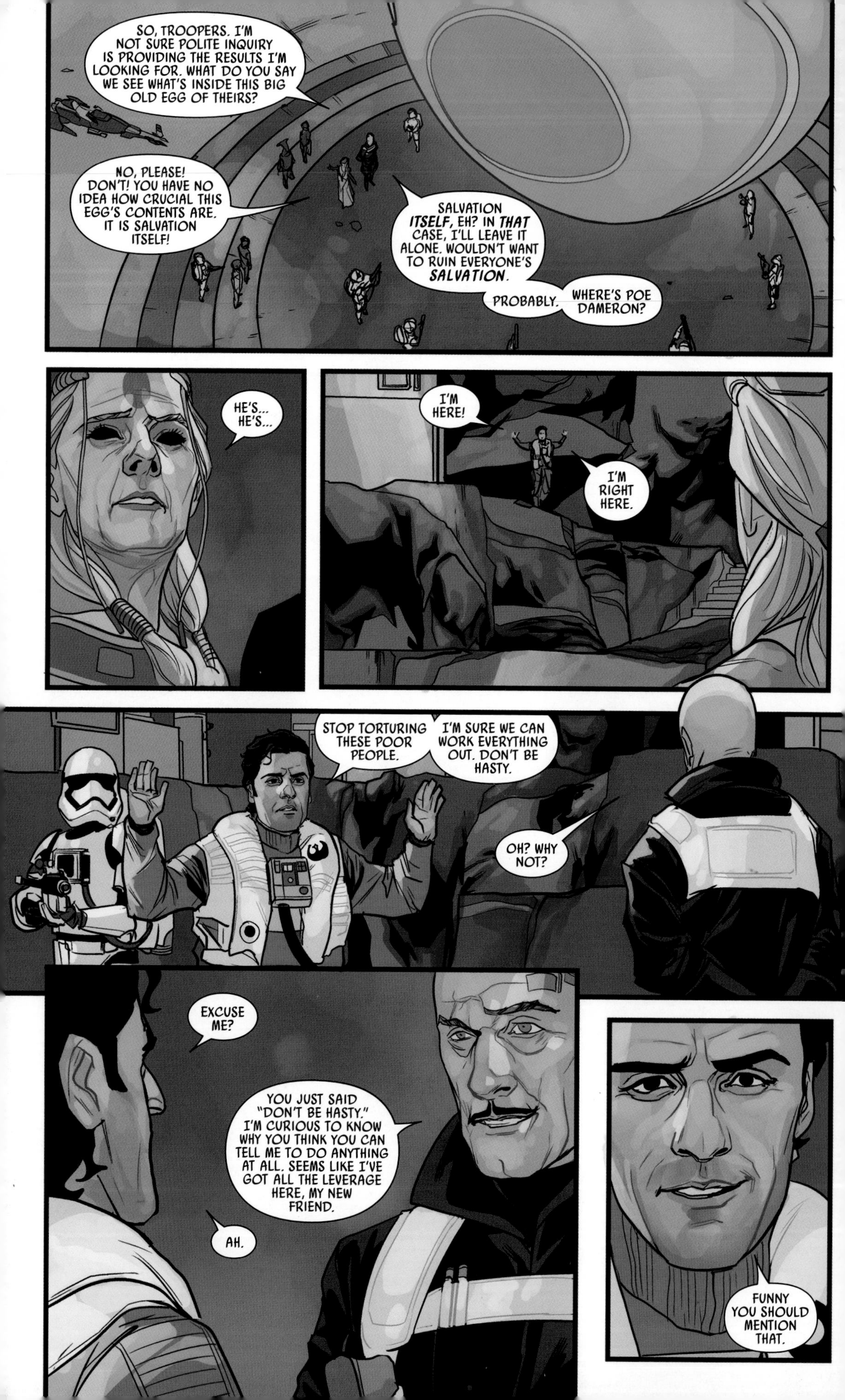
SO, TROOPERS. I'M NOT SURE POLITE INQUIRY IS PROVIDING THE RESULTS I'M LOOKING FOR. WHAT DO YOU SAY WE SEE WHAT'S INSIDE THIS BIG OLD EGG OF THEIRS?
NO, PLEASE! DON'T! YOU HAVE NO IDEA HOW CRUCIAL THIS EGG'S CONTENTS ARE. IT IS SALVATION ITSELF!
SALVATION *ITSELF*, EH? IN *THAT* CASE, I'LL LEAVE IT ALONE. WOULDN'T WANT TO RUIN EVERYONE'S *SALVATION*.
PROBABLY.
WHERE'S POE DAMERON?
HE'S... HE'S...
I'M HERE!
I'M RIGHT HERE.
STOP TORTURING THESE POOR PEOPLE.
I'M SURE WE CAN WORK EVERYTHING OUT. DON'T BE HASTY.
OH? WHY NOT?
EXCUSE ME?
YOU JUST SAID "DON'T BE HASTY." I'M CURIOUS TO KNOW WHY YOU THINK YOU CAN TELL ME TO DO ANYTHING AT ALL. SEEMS LIKE I'VE GOT ALL THE LEVERAGE HERE, MY NEW FRIEND.
AH.
FUNNY YOU SHOULD MENTION THAT.

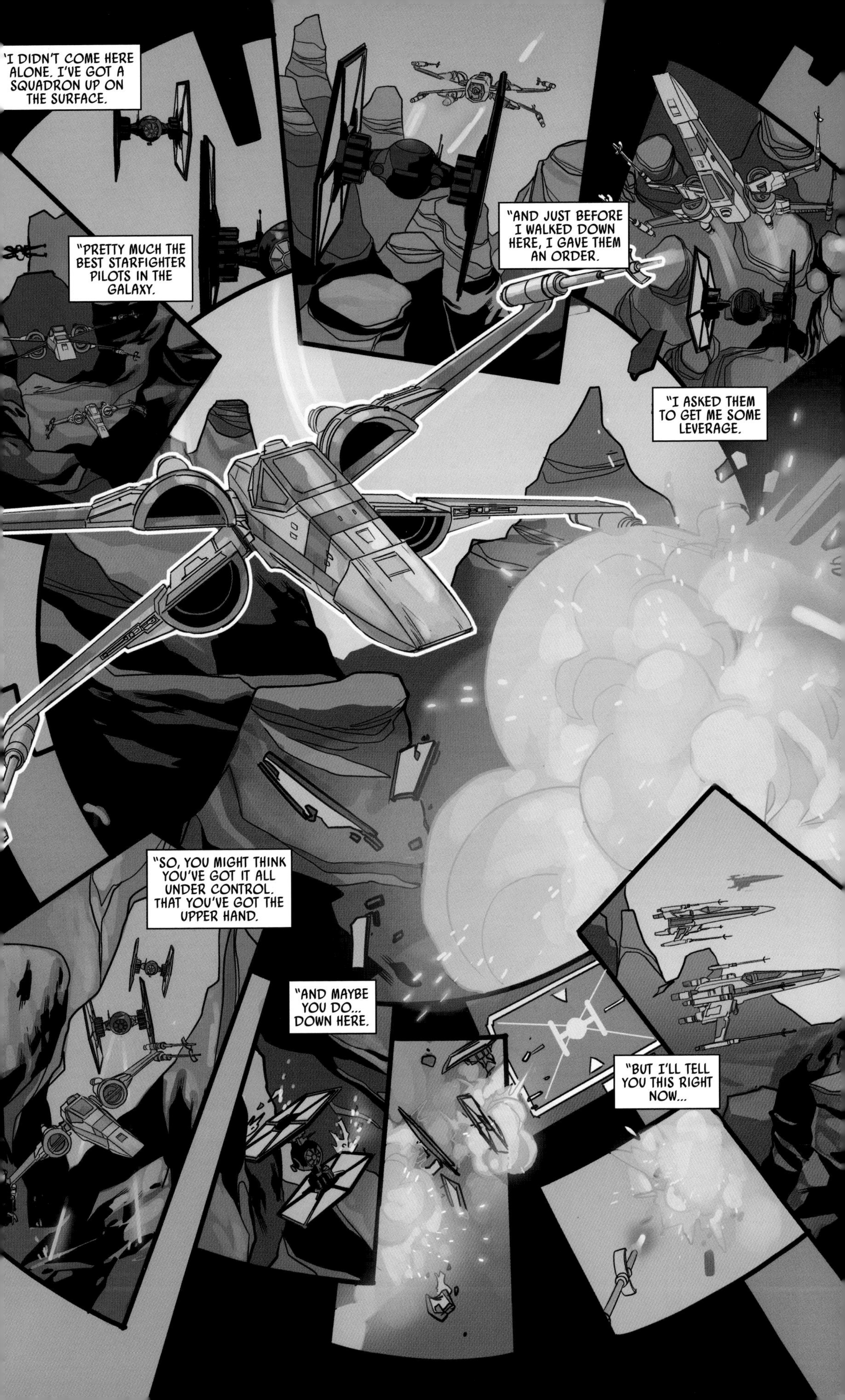
'I DIDN'T COME HERE ALONE. I'VE GOT A SQUADRON UP ON THE SURFACE.
"PRETTY MUCH THE BEST STARFIGHTER PILOTS IN THE GALAXY.
"AND JUST BEFORE I WALKED DOWN HERE, I GAVE THEM AN ORDER.
"I ASKED THEM TO GET ME SOME LEVERAGE.
"SO, YOU MIGHT THINK YOU'VE GOT IT ALL UNDER CONTROL. THAT YOU'VE GOT THE UPPER HAND.
"AND MAYBE YOU DO... DOWN HERE.
"BUT I'LL TELL YOU THIS RIGHT NOW...

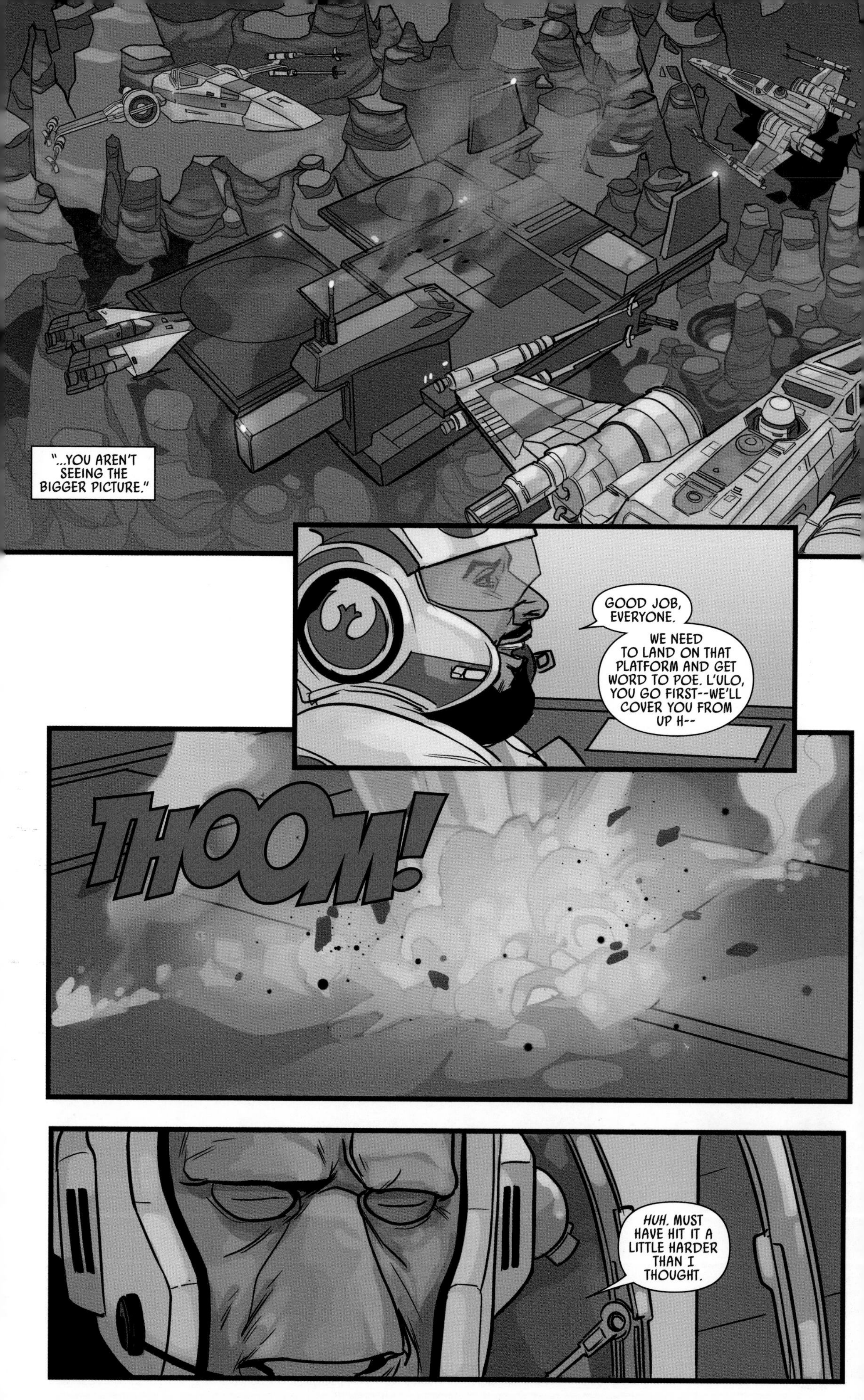
"...YOU AREN'T SEEING THE BIGGER PICTURE."
GOOD JOB, EVERYONE.
WE NEED TO LAND ON THAT PLATFORM AND GET WORD TO POE. L'ULO, YOU GO FIRST--WE'LL COVER YOU FROM UP H--
THOOM!
HUH. MUST HAVE HIT IT A LITTLE HARDER THAN I THOUGHT.

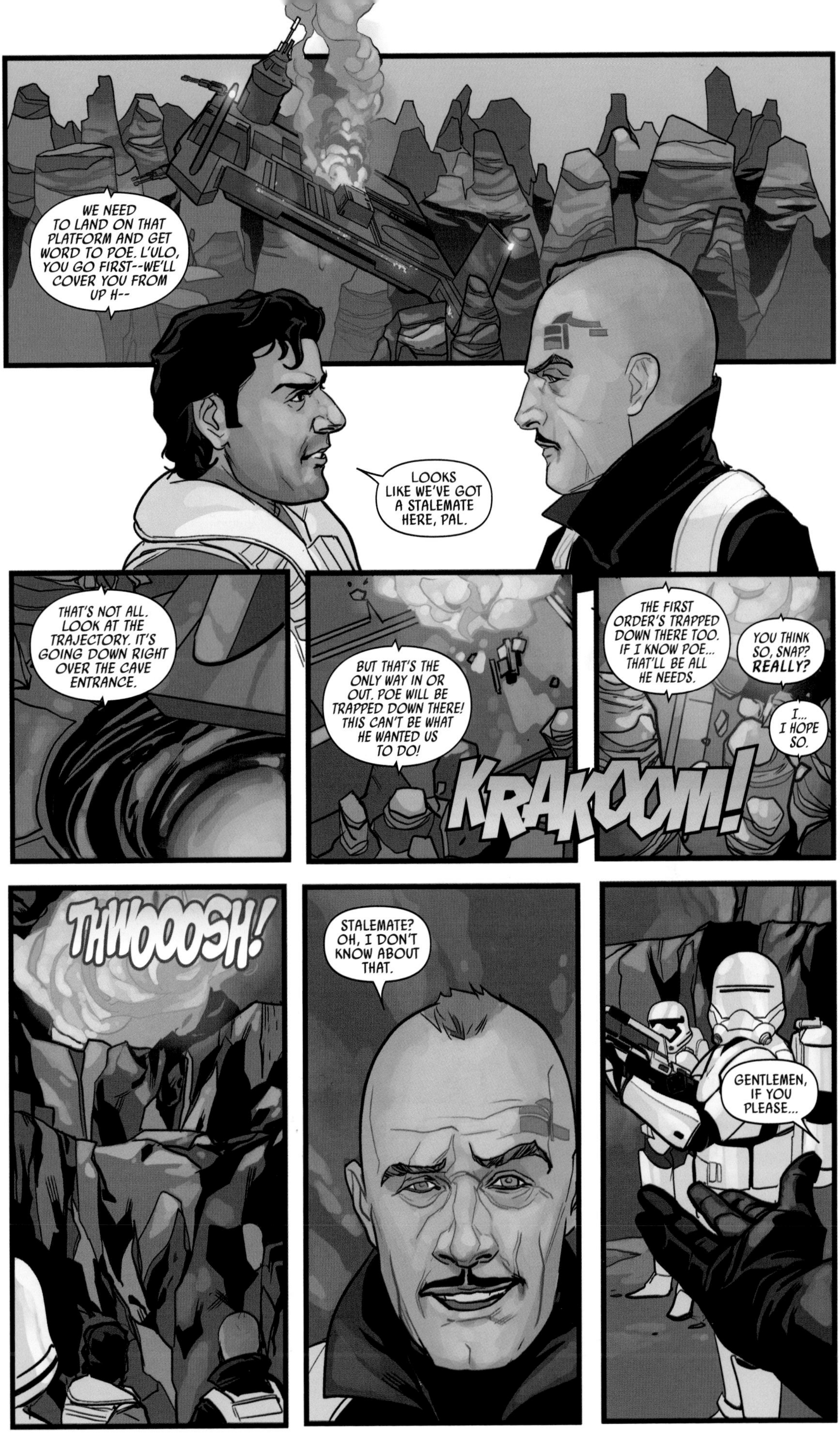
WE NEED TO LAND ON THAT PLATFORM AND GET WORD TO POE. L'ULO, YOU GO FIRST--WE'LL COVER YOU FROM UP H--
LOOKS LIKE WE'VE GOT A STALEMATE HERE, PAL.
THAT'S NOT ALL. LOOK AT THE TRAJECTORY. IT'S GOING DOWN RIGHT OVER THE CAVE ENTRANCE.
BUT THAT'S THE ONLY WAY IN OR OUT. POE WILL BE TRAPPED DOWN THERE! THIS CAN'T BE WHAT HE WANTED US TO DO!
THE FIRST ORDER'S TRAPPED DOWN THERE TOO. IF I KNOW POE... THAT'LL BE ALL HE NEEDS.
YOU THINK SO, SNAP? REALLY?
I... I HOPE SO.
KRAKOOM!
THWOOOSH!
STALEMATE? OH, I DON'T KNOW ABOUT THAT.
GENTLEMEN, IF YOU PLEASE...

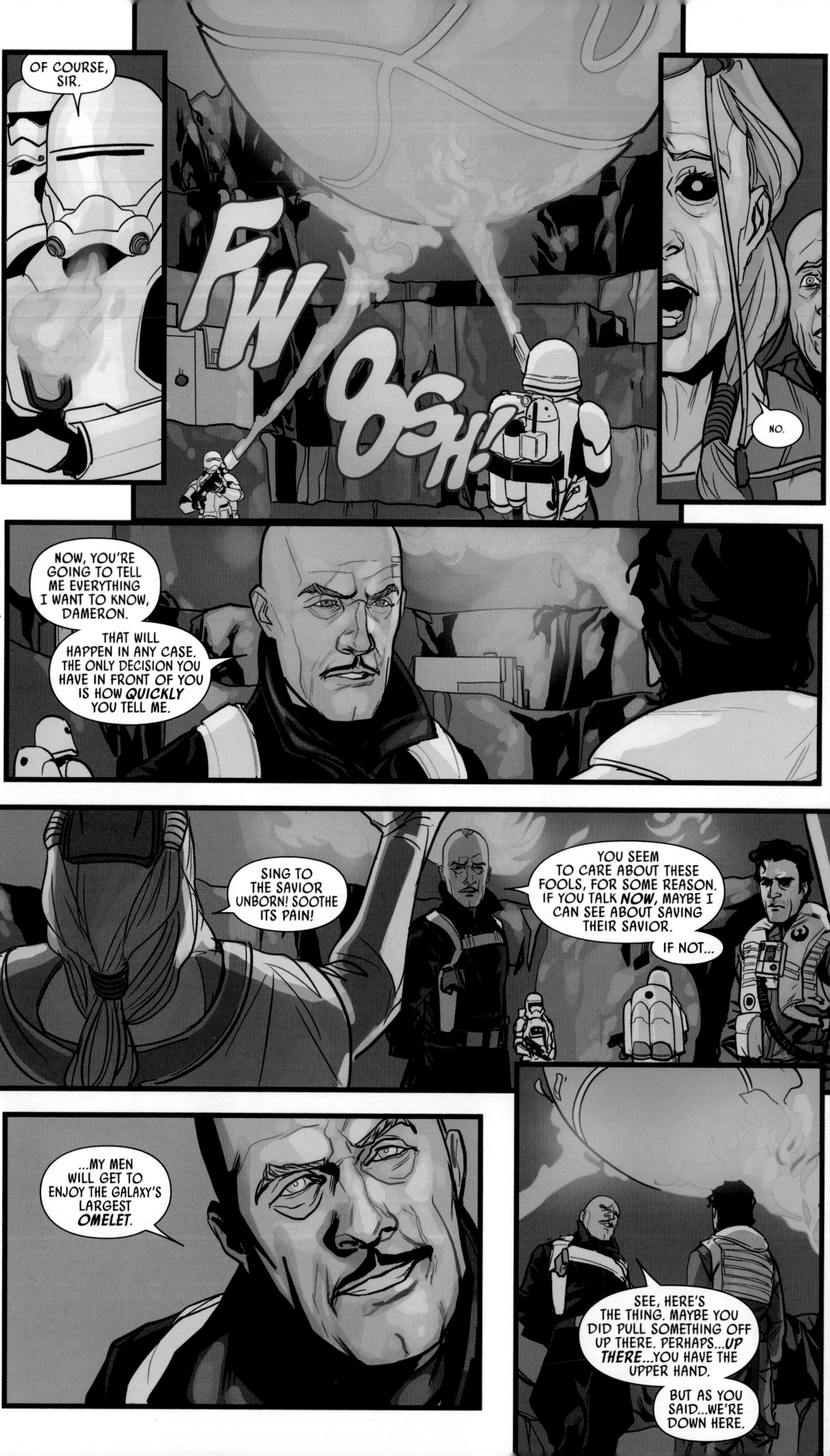
OF COURSE, SIR.
FWOOSH!
NO.
NOW, YOU'RE GOING TO TELL ME EVERYTHING I WANT TO KNOW, DAMERON.
THAT WILL HAPPEN IN ANY CASE. THE ONLY DECISION YOU HAVE IN FRONT OF YOU IS HOW QUICKLY YOU TELL ME.
SING TO THE SAVIOR UNBORN! SOOTHE ITS PAIN!
YOU SEEM TO CARE ABOUT THESE FOOLS, FOR SOME REASON. IF YOU TALK NOW, MAYBE I CAN SEE ABOUT SAVING THEIR SAVIOR.
IF NOT...
...MY MEN WILL GET TO ENJOY THE GALAXY'S LARGEST OMELET.
SEE, HERE'S THE THING. MAYBE YOU DID PULL SOMETHING OFF UP THERE. PERHAPS...UP THERE...YOU HAVE THE UPPER HAND.
BUT AS YOU SAID...WE'RE DOWN HERE.

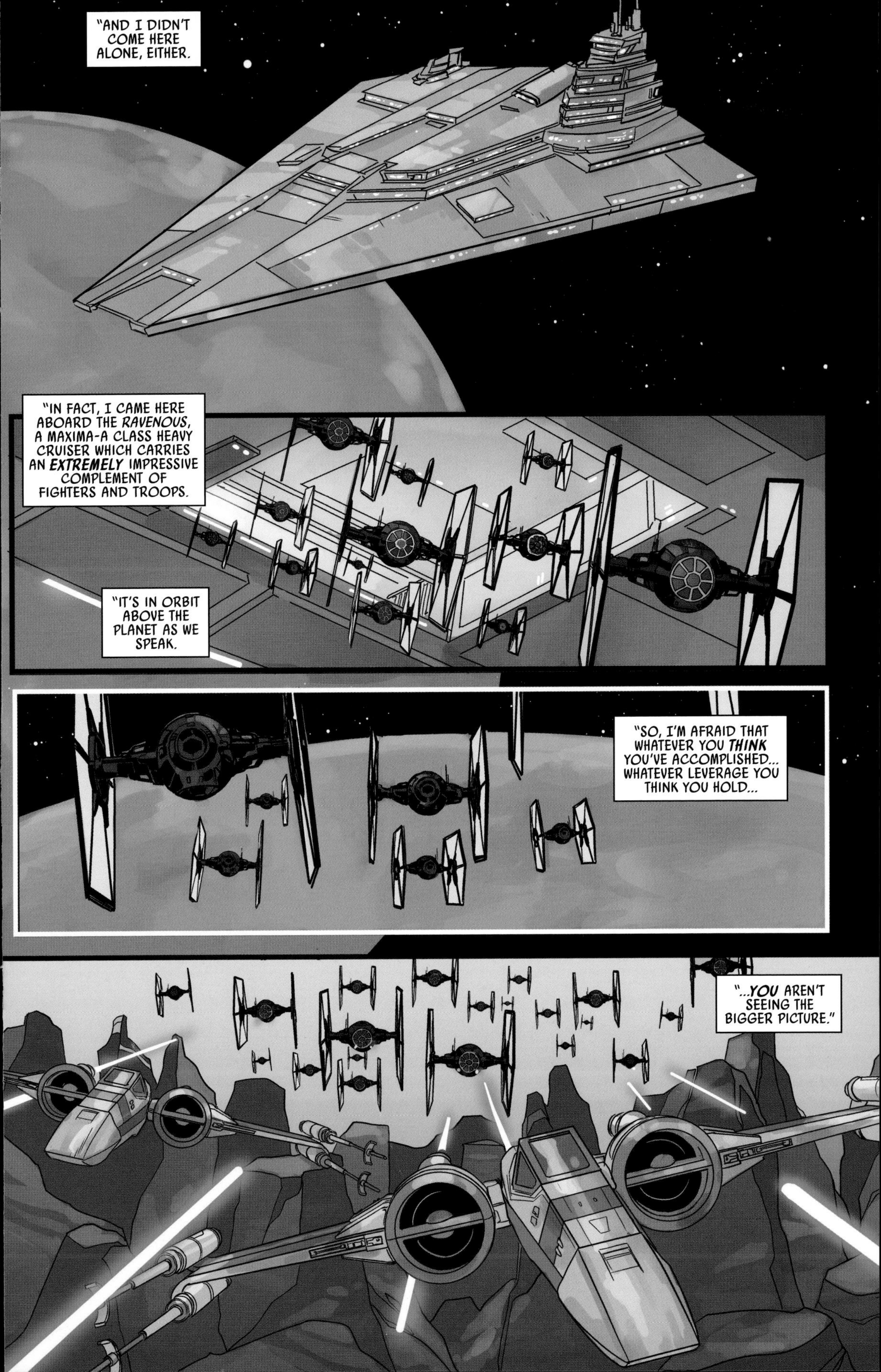
"AND I DIDN'T COME HERE ALONE, EITHER.
"IN FACT, I CAME HERE ABOARD THE *RAVENOUS*, A MAXIMA-A CLASS HEAVY CRUISER WHICH CARRIES AN ***EXTREMELY*** IMPRESSIVE COMPLEMENT OF FIGHTERS AND TROOPS.
"IT'S IN ORBIT ABOVE THE PLANET AS WE SPEAK.
"SO, I'M AFRAID THAT WHATEVER YOU ***THINK*** YOU'VE ACCOMPLISHED... WHATEVER LEVERAGE YOU THINK YOU HOLD...
"...***YOU*** AREN'T SEEING THE BIGGER PICTURE."

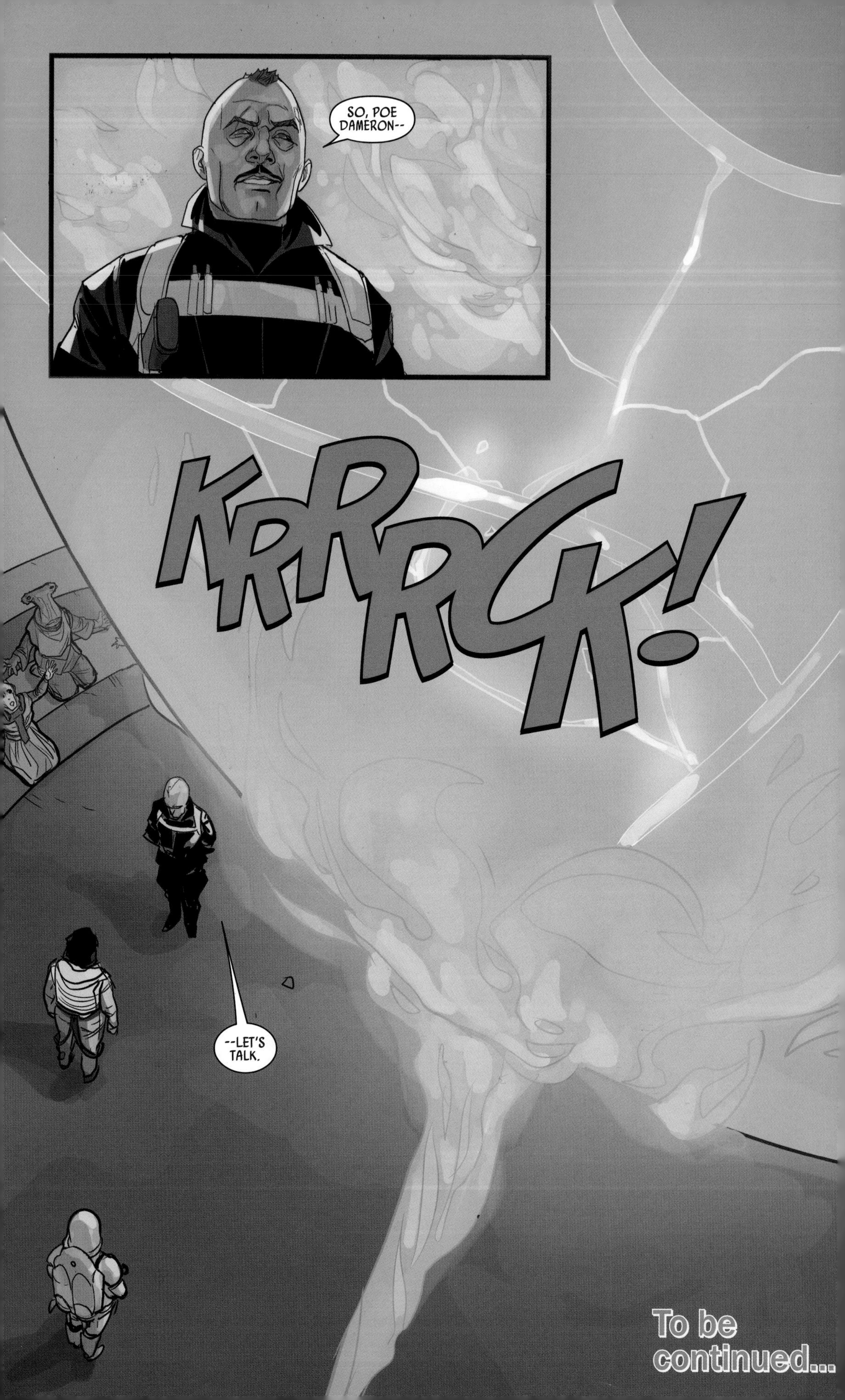
SO, POE DAMERON--
KRRRCK!
--LET'S TALK.
To be continued...

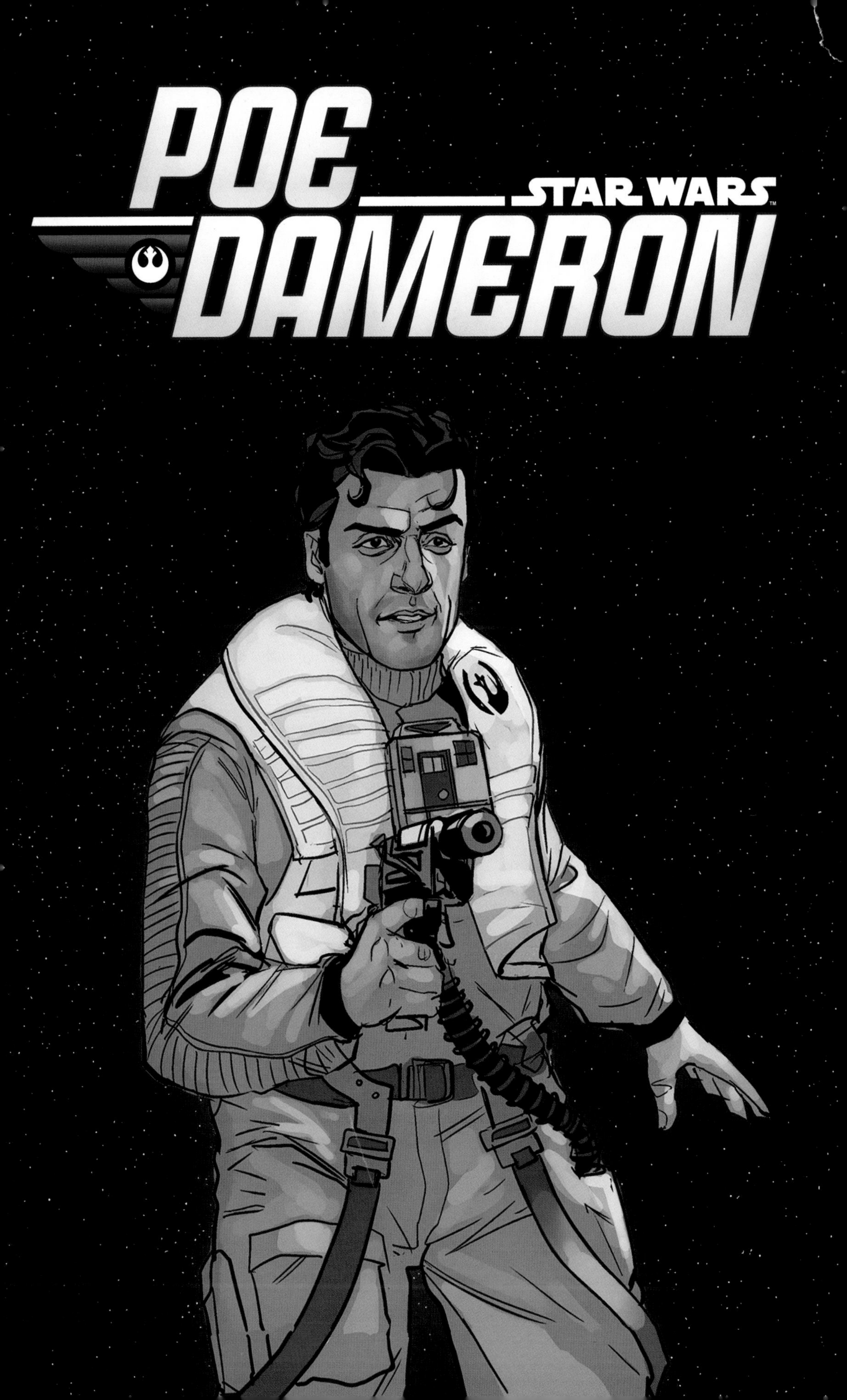
POE
STAR WARS
DAMERON

POE DAMERON
STAR WARS

COLLECT THEM ALL!

Set of 6 Hardcover Books ISBN: 978-1-5321-4133-1

STAR WARS
POE DAMERON
STAR WARS
BLACK SQUADRON: VOLUME 1
SOULE NOTO

Hardcover Book ISBN
978-1-5321-4134-8

STAR WARS
POE DAMERON
STAR WARS
BLACK SQUADRON: VOLUME 2
SOULE NOTO

Hardcover Book ISBN
978-1-5321-4135-5

STAR WARS
POE DAMERON
STAR WARS
BLACK SQUADRON: VOLUME 3
SOULE NOTO

Hardcover Book ISBN
978-1-5321-4136-2

STAR WARS
POE DAMERON
STAR WARS
LOCKDOWN: VOLUME 1
SOULE NOTO

Hardcover Book ISBN
978-1-5321-4137-9

STAR WARS
POE DAMERON
STAR WARS
LOCKDOWN: VOLUME 2
SOULE NOTO

Hardcover Book ISBN
978-1-5321-4138-6

STAR WARS
POE DAMERON
STAR WARS
LOCKDOWN: VOLUME 3
SOULE NOTO

Hardcover Book ISBN
978-1-5321-4139-3

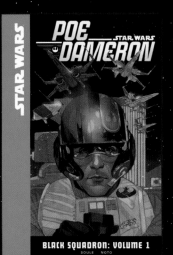

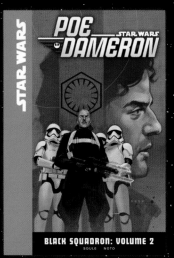

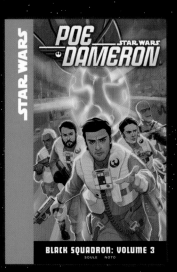

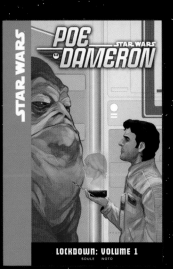

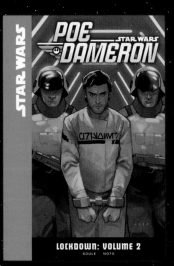

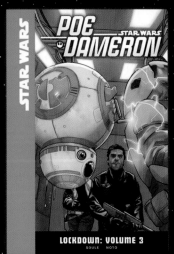